This book is dedicated to all the beautiful animals
and characters who roam around our natural world,
making our lives sparkle.
Any resemblance to my neighbours' pets is purely
coincidental and very Tiny...

What our readers, big and small, say about *Spikey*, the first book in this series

"An enjoyable adventure for children to read or listen to. [...] Delicate illustrations conveying the humour and kindness in the story complete this appealing package." – **The School Librarian**

"This is a charming tale of friendship and teamwork. [...] Through the quiz questions, readers are encouraged to think about how the different characters may be feeling, what they are learning and what could happen next to maintain engagement with the story. The illustrations are [...] another aspect for young readers to delight in." – **Love Reading for Kids**

"An engaging and beautifully illustrated story for young readers about 'Britain's favourite wild mammal'." – **The Association for Science Education,** *Primary Science* **(journal)**

"This story really resonated with the children. They identified with the characters and understood how important both receiving friendship and being a good friend is. The language is child-friendly, but also extends the children's vocabulary. A truly delightful book with thought-provoking issues." – **Sue Colman, teacher at Harlyn Primary School, London, UK**

"It was really funny and I really liked it." – **Maya (seven), UK**

"I loved the details and pictures. I like how Spikey finds friends who like him even if he is a little different." – **Christian (eight), US**

"I always knew that all the animals in parks, gardens and woods were helping each other, but this book is a real confirmation of it! I even think I saw Spikey in our garden the other day. I need to go now to prepare something to eat and drink for him." **– Julie (five), Czech Republic**

"I was sad at the end because I wanted it to be longer. […] My favourite part was when they ate the berries and their lips turned blue. That made me laugh." – **Frankie (seven), UK**

"It was a funny and cool story! I am happy they all became friends in the end and Spikey found himself a home and a place where he felt like he belonged." – **Bentlee (10), US**

"I like the ideas Spikey came up with. Especially the names – he gave names to all his friends and names are very, *very* important." **– Ládík (eight), Czech Republic**

"We all loved it! The questions at the bottom were amazing and really helped my eight-year-old who struggles with book comprehension. And they really made him and my 11-year-old think. And even my two-year-old could answer some of them. The writing was amazing. And the storyline and the characters make you fall in love with them instantly. Can't wait to tell others about it!" – **Miranda Kay, mum of three, US**

"Such an informative and beautifully written book that would be a great addition to any classroom or home library. After reading this story we have now done our bit to help hedgehogs by building a hedgehog hotel in our garden." – **Lisa, mum of two, UK**

SPIKEY

and the Caterpillar Sausage Cat

WRITTEN BY TEREZA HEPBURN

ILLUSTRATED BY MIKE PHILLIPS

For Gordon, the best editor I could have asked for
— thank you!

And for my John, the biggest nature lover and garden
watcher of all time, with all my love.

Throughout the book, the quiz questions on the left-hand pages are for younger readers to answer:

★   What type of animal is White Tip?
★   What can you see in this picture?
★   Who did Spikey say goodbye to?

Introduction

Hello, hello! I'm White Tip or you can call me Mr Fox. I'm not usually a chatty one, but talking about my friend Spikey always makes me smile. I've never met a hedgehog quite like him!

Not long ago, Spikey said goodbye to Grandma Hedgehog and set off to make his way in the world. He wasn't sure if he could make it on his own, but all the other little hedgehogs had left home, and he didn't want to be left behind.

And the questions on the right-hand pages are for older readers to answer, think about or discuss:

- ❋ Why does talking about Spikey make White Tip smile?
- ❋ How did Spikey feel leaving home?
- ❋ What do you like best about this picture?

Spikey was born in Regent's Park, London. It's only a few hundred acres of grass and beautiful trees, but to him, it's the *whole wide world.* He has one back leg shorter and weaker than the other, but this hasn't stopped him, and he's travelled a very long way. Spikey is a very small hedgehog, but he has a very big heart.

If you know as much about hedgehogs as I do, you'll know they love exploring and are really good at getting themselves into all kinds of trouble. Maybe that's why Spikey is also good at helping others who are in trouble? That's how we met and became friends.

I've given him my fox promise that, even when I'm not with Spikey, I'll keep an eye out for him and keep him safe. So does Stripey the ladybird, the other friend he has made. She watches out for him from above. You might not always see us, but we're usually close by, and as his friends, we're with him every step of the way.

★   What is unusual about Spikey?
★   What do hedgehogs like to do?
★   Who keeps an eye out for Spikey? Who keeps an eye out for you?

* Who are Spikey's friends? How do you know?
* What does a friend do for you that other people don't?
* What do you think a 'fox promise' is?

Chapter One

"No! Nooo! Nooooooooooo…"

THUD!

"Ouch! Ouuuch…Ouch!"

The little robin had fallen to the ground and was now trying to sit up. It was really hard for him to sit up in the grass, which was as high as at least three robins sitting on top of each other. He looked around, feeling confused. *It wasn't supposed to be like this*, he thought. *I was supposed to flap my wings and, whooooshhhh, I would be flying! This is bad; this is really bad! In fact, it might be very bad!* He realised he had fluffed himself up – and robins *never* fluff up. Some robins believe that they are in charge of the world. All of it!

★ What had happened to the robin? Why?

★ What do you think 'fluff up' means?

★ What do you think is happening in the picture on page 13? How do you know?

He was just realising he was really proud to be a robin when he heard some rustling in the grass – and robins don't rustle. *What could that be?*

Oh no. Oh nooo! It's coming towards me! I need to hide – and quickly – but where should I hide? Where? Part of him was thinking robins never hide, and another part of him was looking left and right, up and down, backwards and forwards, and round and round and round and round and round and round, trying to find somewhere to hide.

How would you explain what had happened to the robin?

Do you think robins are in charge of the world? Why?

How would you describe this robin, using the words and the picture here?

Spikey

Deep in the long grass, Spikey was rustling around. Hedgehogs love to rustle. It's really good fun. Rustle, rustle, rustle, rustle! He had sniffed and snuffled his way across the park all morning, without meeting anyone or seeing anything. He began to feel worried. *Suppose I'm out here all alone in this big, wide world forever?* he thought, a shiver running down his spikey spine. Then, suddenly, a really loud noise made him jump.

★ What was Spikey doing?
★ What noises did the robin make?
★ What are all of the things that happened to Spikey's nose?

"*ACHOOO!*" The little robin sneezed so heartily that the large green-and-red leaf he was trying to hide under blew off over his head.

Spikey's nose twitched and then continued twitching more and more – first with fear and then with excitement. Looking ahead, he could see a tiny bird lying on its back in front of him, struggling to get up. "Are you OK?" asked Spikey.

The tiny bird fluffed up its feathers again and exploded into a shrill noise: "Wheep, wheep, *wheeeep, WHEEEEEEEP!*"

Then, *CLOP!*

"*Oooowwww!*" howled Spikey as he fell backwards with shock into the long grass. His beautiful, long nose had been clopped! And it hurt! He started to roll up into a ball, struggling to hold back the tears (yes, it really had hurt that much!).

---

* What emotions did Spikey feel? Why?
* Have you ever felt these emotions? When?
* What do you think about the robin's behaviour? Why did the robin do these things?

Spikey could see the small robin bouncing around in the grass and so he pulled himself together. "Why would you do that?" he asked crossly. "Why would you peck me? And on my nose – at the very end! I didn't do anything bad to you!"

"I...I...I don't know. You look dangerous. And this is my leaf to hide under, so don't try to squeeze in. Don't even come close! Keep your distance so I don't have to peck you again. I'm warning you!" the robin added as he tried to cover himself with the leaf again.

Spikey looked confused. "But if I just *look* dangerous, how do you know I actually *am* dangerous? By the way, I can still see your brown legs!"

The robin put the leaf down and stuck out his bright-red chest. "I'm Reginald," he said. "But you can call me Reggie."

★   What were some of the things the robin did?

★   How would you describe Reggie in the picture?

★   Do you like Reggie? Why?

Spikey

"And I'm Spikey," the little hedgehog replied in his friendliest voice.

"Cheerio, Spikey," Reggie chirped, walking off in a wobbly manner.

"Shouldn't you be flying?"

"I'm a robin and I can travel any way I want!"

If you were Spikey, what would you have done?

How would you describe Spikey in the picture?

Do you like Spikey? Why?

As Reggie hobbled off, Spikey noticed the bird's soft, fluffy feathers. He thought to himself, *Reggie's a baby robin. He must have fallen out of his nest and can't get back because he hasn't learned to fly yet!* "Well, I just thought that if you're so keen to get away from me, flying would have been much quicker," Spikey then said, playing along.

The robin ignored this remark and continued to hobble away. Spikey started to feel sorry for him. "Here, let me help you," he called, rushing to catch up with the tiny creature. It wasn't easy. Spikey's shorter back leg felt tired and was starting to hurt.

"Go away!" said Reggie rudely. "I don't want your company. I'm perfectly fine by myself." The baby bird was now thinking about his mummy and how she had explained to him that there are some big creatures out there with four legs who will eat anything. He had definitely counted four legs on this

---

★ Do you think Reggie is a baby robin? Why?

★ Why was Spikey tired?

★ Do you think Reggie deserved a second chance? Why?

one. So he kept marching away, not looking back and holding his chest out. He wanted to look brave, but really, he was *very* scared!

Why is this robin being so difficult? I need to give him another chance. Everybody deserves a second chance, thought Spikey, so he ran after the little bird. "You're not fine, Reggie," he called. "You're in real danger if you can't fly away. May I help you to fly?"

Reggie carried on marching away for a while, then he stopped and turned round. "I'm thinking about what you said just now about helping me learn to fly. How would you do that?" he asked.

Spikey just smiled, then he sat the little robin on a big, strong leaf, gripped the stem in his teeth, and managed to drag Reggie up a short slope to a flat, sandy ledge. "Now jump off and flap your wings as hard as you can," he urged.

:: Why did Reggie keep walking away? Was he right to do that?

:: If you were Reggie, what would you have done?

:: If you were Spikey, what would you have done?

Spikey

★ How would you describe the picture?
★ What does 'once again' tell you? What has been happening?
★ Why is Reggie so upset?

THUD! The little bird crash-landed once again. "This is *your* fault!" he groaned.

"No, it's not," Spikey replied calmly. "Your wings aren't fully grown because you're too young to fly."

"Well, that's where you're wrong, pointy face! I'm the same age as my brothers and sisters, and they can all fly." Reggie paused and sniffed. "I just haven't quite got the hang of it yet, OK?"

Out of the blue, a deep voice came from under their feet.

How does Spikey look in the picture? Why?

How would you describe Reggie's behaviour?

Do you have any advice for Reggie and Spikey?

"Who's there?" it bellowed.

The next moment, the earth in front of Spikey and Reggie started to move and a head popped up from underground. It was followed by the body of a worm – possibly the biggest worm in the history of all worms.

"I'm Dave," the huge worm said with a friendly smile. "What are you two doin' 'ere, apart from thumpin' on the ground an' disturbin' my shut-eye?"

"We're trying to get Reginald here to fly," explained the little hedgehog. "I'm Spikey, by the way."

"That sounds cool, Spikey! May I 'elp? It gets kinda borin' down there in the darkness, ya know."

Spikey nodded. He no longer felt worried or sad. He had two new friends and something very important to do today.

★   What is happening in the picture?
★   How would you describe Dave?
★   What does Dave think about being underground in the darkness?

Spikey

---

* Do you think Dave is happy? Why?
* How does Spikey feel?
* What do you think will happen next? Why?

Chapter Two

"Well, come on, then," Reggie urged impatiently. "If one of you is going to help me fly, hurry up and get on with it!"

"Would ya like to go first?" Dave asked Spikey.

"No thanks. I've tried once already," Spikey answered quickly. *I haven't got the faintest idea what to do this time – but nobody must know that!* "You go first, Dave."

★ What does 'impatiently' mean?
★ What does 'I haven't got the faintest idea' mean?
★ What is an otter? How is the worm like an otter?

"Thanks, mate," called the gigantic worm, starting to burrow into the ground. "I've got a crackin' idea 'ow to 'elp sort out this flyin' problem."

Spikey and Reggie watched and waited as Dave continued to make holes in the ground, diving down each time and then surfacing again like an otter coming up for air.

"What exactly are you doing?" Reggie asked with a weary sigh and a big yawn. "I'm bored to tears!"

"You just 'ang in there, little birdie," answered Dave. "I've nearly finished. I've just gotta give this patch of ground another goin' over, an' it'll all be ready for ya."

- Why is the little robin impatient?
- Why does Spikey not want anyone to know that he hasn't got the faintest idea?
- What do you think Dave is doing?

Spikey

Dave had dug and redug a circle of sandy earth underneath the ledge that Spikey had used before. The ground was now soft and loose, like a feather bed, only it was made of soil. "This'll stop ya 'urtin' yerself, mate!" the big worm explained excitedly.

"I don't have a clue what you're sayin', Dayve," said Reggie, copying the worm's London accent. "If you're going to speak to me, kindly do so in words I can understand."

Sensing a quarrel brewing, Spikey jumped in quickly: "I think Dave means that, if you don't manage to fly, you'll have a nice, soft landing and not hurt yourself like you did before."

★ What is happening in the picture?

★ What has Dave been doing?

★ What will happen next?

"Well, why didn't he say that?" argued the little robin.

"I did!" Dave protested.

Spikey was already dragging another large leaf towards his new friends. "Come on, Reginald, hop on," he said eagerly. "I'll pull you up to the ledge, and you can practise flying as many times as you like now. You have Dave's special cushion to keep you safe."

Which words are hard for you to read or understand?

Can you find out more about these words in a dictionary?

How would you explain what has happened on pages 26 and 27?

All of a sudden, Reggie got the idea. "I see! Thank you, Dave," he said politely. "This is clearly the answer to my problem!" Spikey dragged him up the slope, and the robin launched himself off the ledge without a care in the world. "Look! I'm flying!" he called, flapping each of his wings at different times and speeds.

"No, you're not!" cried Spikey. "You're falling fast!"

"It doesn't matter." Reggie chuckled. "I'll have a nice, soft landing…"

THUD!

The little robin hit the ground to one side of the safety cushion. The wind had blown him off course, and he missed the circle of soft, churned-up earth.

"Are ya all right?" Dave called anxiously.

"Of course I'm not all right!" shouted Reggie. "I now have even more aches and pains than I did before. But never mind. And it doesn't matter that I

★ How does Reggie's face change in the pictures on page 29?

★ What has happened to Reggie?

★ What does 'anxiously' mean?

don't understand what you're saying, because I shall never speak to you again – *ever!"* With that, the little robin turned his back on Dave angrily.

***

° Do you think Spikey and Dave are good teachers? Why?

° How does Reggie feel? Do you agree?

° What do you think will happen next?

After this accident, Spikey tried frantically to think of another way to get Reggie airborne. He was about to give up and say he was sorry for not keeping his promise when he spotted a small child's kite tumbling past with its string dangling behind it. The kite had obviously been lost or left behind, because nobody was following it, and it was just being blown backwards and forwards by the gusty wind. *This is the answer!* Spikey thought excitedly, and he hurried across to grab the trailing string in his teeth. He dragged the kite back to his friends, not telling them where it had come from. He wanted them to think he'd been planning this all along. "OK, Dave," he called cheerily. "My turn now!"

Spikey asked Dave to wrap the kite string round his tail while he himself gripped it in his teeth and with his paws.

★ What does 'tried frantically to think' mean? Has this ever happened to you?

★ Do you think Spikey will give up? Why?

★ Why does Spikey say, "Mmm mm mmm mmm-mmm..."?

"Mmm mm mmm mmm-mmm mmm mm mmm mm mm mmm m mmmm," he told Reggie.

The little robin rolled his eyes upwards. "Not you as well," he groaned. "I can't understand what you're saying either."

Spikey let go of the string. "I said, 'Jump on the wooden bit and sit on it like a perch.'"

"Why?"

"Because..." began Spikey, then he gripped the string in his mouth again. "Mmm...mmm...mmmm!"

But Reggie understood and hopped onto the perch.

Suddenly, the wind caught the kite and lifted it high into the air.

"Wow!" gasped Reggie. "This feels just like flying!"

What do you think of Spikey's problem-solving skills?

Spikey promised to help Reggie to fly. Do you think he will keep his promise? Why?

The wind has caught the kite and lifted it high into the air. What do you think will happen next?

Spikey

Spikey continued to let out the kite, and Reggie went higher and higher, but the string kept jerking in Spikey's mouth and made his teeth ache. So, he wound the last bit round his paws and clung on to Dave so both of them were holding the kite down firmly.

"What do we do now, mate?" asked Dave.

"Nothing," Spikey replied. "Just let Reggie get a good feel of being in the sky, and then pull him back down...*Whoa!*"

A particularly strong gust of wind unexpectedly lifted Spikey and Dave right off the ground! They sailed up into the air as if they'd made a gigantic leap.

Reggie peered down over the kite frame. "Are you two getting the feel of flying as well?" he called happily.

"No, we're not!" yelled Dave.

"He means yes; yes, we are," Spikey shouted back hastily.

★ What is happening in the picture?
★ How are Reggie, Spikey and Dave feeling in the picture?
★ What has just happened to Reggie, Spikey and Dave?

Spikey

✱ Look at the picture. What do Reggie, Spikey and Dave's faces tell
you about how they are feeling?

✱ Point to all the words on page 32 that are the hardest to read and
understand. How can you find out what these words mean?

✱ Why is the kite string no longer in Spikey's mouth?

Spikey

Having sailed so high that his feet and Dave's tail were brushing the tree-tops, the wind dropped suddenly, and the kite drifted downwards at an ever-increasing speed. The three helpless flyers found themselves heading straight down towards a big patch of prickly bushes. Luckily, they just managed to skim over the top of these and landed on some soft, squishy, red ground beside them.

"What *is* this?" demanded Dave.

"Fallen fruit," Spikey explained. "Raspberries, to be precise. We've landed in the middle of a patch of ripe raspberries."

The delicious smell of the squashed fruit and the taste of the sweet, red juice reminded everyone they hadn't eaten for ages and were very hungry. So Spikey and Dave freed themselves from the kite string, and everyone tucked in, gobbling up the berries until they were full.

★   How high did the three friends fly?
★   What did the three friends land in?
★   What is happening in the picture?

Spikey

"Thank you for this, Spikey," said Reggie, his chest now stained *doubly red* from the raspberry juice.

"My pleasure," Spikey replied. "I thought we all deserved a delicious treat after a hard morning of practising how to fly."

Dave knew Spikey hadn't planned this and looked at him sharply, but the hedgehog winked back at him while sinking his teeth into yet another big raspberry. Spikey was enjoying being in charge, and it made him feel proud and confident. *Nothing else can go wrong now. This is going to be the best day of my life!*

How did the three friends feel when they landed?

Did Spikey plan to land in the raspberries?

Why did Spikey wink at Dave? Do you think Spikey is being a good friend just now? Why?

Chapter Three

Spikey, Reggie and Dave felt very tired after their hard morning's work and big feast. Yawning loudly, they made their way to a shady spot under the bushes and curled up together for a snooze. It was getting on for teatime when they woke up, but it was high summer and wouldn't get dark for many hours yet.

"I fink I'll go 'ome," said Dave.

Spikey made a doubting face. "It'll be a very long walk...or should I say wriggle? We flew a great distance on that kite!"

★   What do 'feast', 'shady', 'curled' and 'snooze' mean?

★   How do the three friends feel?

★   How does Dave travel around?

"It doesn't bother me, bro," Dave said with a grin. "I can take a shortcut underground."

Spikey and Reggie looked at each other with puzzled frowns as Dave dived head first into a hole in the ground and disappeared. He popped his head up again from another hole a bit further on to explain. "Under 'ere, we worms 'ave dug loads of tunnels that criss-cross under the park. So ya can slither down 'em in any direction ya like an' get to where yer goin' in the eye of a blink."

"What?" said Reggie and Spikey together.

"Oh, sorry. Wrong way round! I wriggle down the tunnels in the blink of an eye."

Can you point to all the words on pages 36 and 37 that you are not quite sure of, and ask for help with these?

Pick three of these words. What new sentence can you make up for each one?

What do you think Dave is saying to Reggie in this picture?

★ How would you describe the picture?

★ What has happened to Reggie?

★ Why did this happen? What advice would you give to the three friends?

Dave's friends were too busy laughing at his mistake to notice the worm had suddenly gone very pale and was slithering back towards them. *"Look out, mate! Look out!"* Dave yelled, but it was too late.

Something big and tabby, with brown circles on both sides of its tummy and white socks on its feet, leapt forward and took Reggie in its mouth.

"Help! *Heeeelp!* Somebody help me, *please!"* squawked the terrified robin.

---

* What has just happened, and what will happen next?
* Do you think the cat is really wearing white socks?
* Why do people sometimes describe things (such as 'wearing white socks') in different ways? Do you like this? Why?

Reggie had been caught by a cat. And it wasn't just any cat – it was a very *big* cat! Spikey and Dave were frozen with fear. The three friends had been having such a good time together that they hadn't given a thought to the potential dangers.

Dave was the first to regain his senses. The cat had run off with Reggie in its mouth, so the worm dived down his wormhole to follow underground. "That's Tiny, the park ranger's cat," he called to Spikey before he disappeared. "She'll be goin' frough the Rose Garden to the house."

I know where the Rose Garden is, thought Spikey. *I went there with Stripey and White Tip the other day. I can't really see it as I don't have very good eyesight, but I can smell where it is. It's over there in the distance.*

★   What is the cat called?

★   Where is the cat going? How do you know?

★   Can Spikey see well? How does Spikey get around?

Spikey

A few days before, White Tip had jumped easily through the long grass and hedges when Spikey had been riding on his back, but this time the little hedgehog was on his own and couldn't risk getting lost. So he set off in a straight line across the park. After his afternoon nap, his weaker back leg felt strong at first, but it soon grew tired and started to throb, slowing Spikey down. He could see Dave was already there, waiting at the entrance to the garden and calling to him to hurry. Gritting his teeth against the pain, he ran the rest of the way as fast as he could and then collapsed in a heap beside his friend.

"W-W-Where are they?" he gasped.

"Just round the corner in the garden," Dave replied grimly.

/ ✲ Can you count all the unusual or difficult or interesting words on pages 40 and 41?

/ ✲ Can you find out what these words mean?

/ ✲ Why do Spikey and Dave follow Tiny? Is this a good idea?

* What is happening in the picture?
* What does Spikey call Tiny?
* How would you describe Tiny?

Creeping around the gate, they saw Reggie was pinned down by one of the cat's front paws. He was flapping and squawking, clearly unable to get away.

"At least he's alive," murmured Spikey.

"Not for much longer, unless we do somethin' about it." Dave sounded really worried.

After looking at each other and nodding, the pair of them moved forwards with the only weapon available to them – words!

"I've never seen a cat before," announced Spikey, "but you look more like a caterpillar. Are you a caterpillar cat?"

"Nah," Dave chipped in. "Looks more like a long sausage to me."

"OK, then," Spikey agreed in a loud voice. "This creature must be a caterpillar sausage cat!"

How do Reggie, Tiny, Spikey and Dave feel in the picture?

Do you think it's a good idea for Spikey to call Tiny names? Why?

What will happen next?

When Tiny heard what Spikey and Dave were calling her, she got herself all fluffed up and ready to fight, but she didn't attack straight away. *If I do, I shall lose this bird and my dinner with it, she thought. At the same time, I'm the boss around here, and nobody's allowed to be rude to me. Hmm…maybe I can have it both ways?* So, still holding Reggie firmly with a massive front paw, Tiny turned to the hedgehog and worm with a vicious look on her face. "I can't believe you said that to me," she hissed furiously. "I am Tiny, the park ranger's cat. I am *not* a caterpillar cat and I'm definitely *not* a sausage cat. Who are you to laugh at me? And how *dare* you call me names!"

Despite both of them feeling terrified inside, Spikey and Dave knew they had to continue standing up to this angry creature.

"Reggie is our friend," said Spikey firmly. "You'd better let him go."

★ Why was Tiny 'fluffed up and ready to fight'?
★ How does Tiny describe herself?
★ What do you think Reggie is thinking? Why?

"And why would I do that?" Tiny asked in a cunning voice. "This is my dinner, and I *don't* want to share it."

"Excuse me," Reggie piped up, his voice sounding even higher after having been squashed. "How many times do I need to say this today? I'm Reginald the robin, and I am *not* anyone's dinner! I'm perfectly fine and ready to leave—*uurgh!*"

Reggie's brave speech was cut short by a hard press from Tiny's paw. Then she suddenly flipped Reggie into the air and caught him in her mouth. It was clear she was about to eat him!

"*No!*" shouted Spikey.

"*Please* don't!" begged Reggie.

"*Ya CAN'T!*" yelled Dave. *"This is bang out of order!"*

Why is Tiny so angry?

What does 'cunning' mean? What do you think Tiny will do next? Why?

Is Reggie brave? Why do you think this?

"I have no idea what that means, worm," growled Tiny, with Reggie still in her mouth, "but you can't stop me doing anything I want – so I can and I will."

The next moment, Spikey heard the voice of Mr McDougall, the park ranger, calling the cat's name. *"Come on, Tiny, it's supper time,"* the man shouted, banging a spoon against the side of her bowl. *"Fish and chicken – your favourite – and you've got a whole tin!"*

Everything changed in an instant. Tiny tossed Reggie aside and scampered off, much preferring a big meal of tasty cat food to one small mouthful of bone and feathers.

"Phew! That was close," Dave gasped, and he wriggled over to ask if Reggie was OK.

★　What is Tiny's favourite food?
★　What is happening in the picture?
★　Is Reggie safe?

Spikey

"Of course I'm OK," the robin answered sharply. "It takes more than being in a cat's mouth for five minutes to bother me!"

✴ Who saved Reggie?

✴ Can you guess what everyone is saying in the picture?

✴ What do you think of Reggie now? And what do you think of Spikey?

Reggie then turned to Spikey and put his wings on his hips; he looked *very* cross. "I don't know what you're so pleased about, snuffle boy. You still haven't kept your promise."

Spikey looked confused. "What do you mean?"

"OK, I've been for a ride in the sky, and I know what it feels like to be off the ground – but I still can't fly, can I? I can't flap my wings and take off into the air like my brothers and sisters can. You haven't helped me one little bit, and I'm no nearer being able to fly myself than I was this morning."

All of a sudden, Reggie's brave words stopped. He hid his head under one wing and sobbed so loudly that his whole body shook.

★ Why did Reggie call Spikey 'snuffle boy'?
★ How does Reggie feel in the picture? Why?
★ What will happen next?

- How does Spikey feel?
- Is Reggie being fair?
- If Reggie and Spikey were your friends, what would you say to them? Why?

Chapter Four

Spikey and Dave sat at a respectful distance and waited patiently for Reggie to stop crying. It took a long time, because whenever they thought he'd stopped, he gave another few breathless gasps and sobs. When he was quiet, they went over to where he was lying on the ground and peeped under his wing.

"Are you OK?" Spikey asked kindly.

"I've been OK all along." Reggie replied. He looked up at his two friends and his eyes started to fill with tears again.

Spikey gave the little robin a moment and then said, "Reggie, I'm *so* proud of you. You escaped the cat. You're a hero! When you're ready, we'd love to help you to fly."

★ Why did Spikey and Dave give Reggie time and space to cry?

★ Has Reggie been OK all along?

★ What are Reggie's great strengths?

Reggie took his time and gathered his thoughts. *Spikey is so kind. Maybe this is what friendship means?*

"You're safe now, little one," Spikey continued softly, "but now you see why birds need to fly. Otherwise, this is what happens. You can be in great danger at any time!" Spikey could see Reggie was sitting up straight with an interested look on his face, so he kept talking. "We all have our strengths. Dave can grow long and strong, dig deep and stay safe, and add air to the soil. I usually curl up tight with my sharp spines sticking out to stay safe and I keep the countryside clean. You, mighty robin, can fly and be safe, and then help everyone with your bravery. We all have our strengths, and today, we will work on yours."

Why did Spikey and Dave think Reggie was so brave?

Have you ever helped someone who was upset? What happened?

What are your strengths?

Reggie listened carefully to Spikey's words. "I'll learn to fly so well that I'll teach every robin in the world how to be safe!" Reggie exclaimed. "I'll be the strongest flying robin Regent's Park has ever seen! So come on, let's get on with it again!"

Dave started to wriggle around Reggie, moving the little bird's head left and right and up and down, lifting his right wing and lifting his left wing, and pulling one leg and then the other leg. He also checked Reggie's feathers thoroughly. "Look, I'm a great measurer, an' there's no reason why ya can't fly, mate. Yer fit enough. Yer wings an' feathers 'ave all grown strong an' there's nuffin' stoppin' ya. The problem is that ya don't *fink* ya can do it! So ya need to focus more on what ya *can* do an' stop worryin' about what ya *can't* do."

Ha! That's what it is! thought Spikey. *Reggie is so stroppy because he doesn't want anyone to know he doesn't believe in himself. He just needs lots of*

★   What did Dave do to Reggie's head? Was this a good idea?
★   What did Dave think was stopping Reggie from flying? Do you agree?
★   How did Reggie feel when Spikey believed in him?

encouragement. So Spikey turned to the little bird with a smile. "When I left home," he said, "I was *so* scared! No other hedgehogs helped me when I was out there all on my own with only three strong legs, but I had to try. Then I met my new friends: White Tip the fox and Stripey the ladybird. They were really kind to me – and so much fun to be with! Well, now you've met Dave and me, you're not on your own any more either. We know how difficult it is for you to overcome your fear, but Dave and I really believe in you and know that you can fly!"

"You both really think so?" asked Reggie, double-checking his wings. "Well, maybe, just maybe, today will be my day. But if not, there's always tomorrow, isn't there?" And with that, the young robin started looking around for somewhere to jump off again.

- Why did Dave focus on Reggie's strengths when he spoke to him?
- Have you ever tried and failed at something? Did you try again afterwards? Why?
- Why did Reggie say that if he didn't fly today, he'd try to fly again tomorrow? Do you agree with this?

"Spikey! Spikey! I've been looking for you!" a voice suddenly called from above. "What are you up to today? And who are you with?" It was Stripey, the ladybird, who was circling above their heads and turning somersaults in the air.

"Stripey!" exclaimed Spikey. "It's *so* good to see you! Everyone, this is Stripey, my lovely ladybird friend. And Stripey, this is Reginald and Dave, my two new friends. We are teaching Reggie to fly, you see. And thinking about it, we could do with your help."

"Really? Well, let me see what I can do!" Stripey flew down and landed on the grass. She then put two of her six legs on her hips as she looked the robin up and down.

"OK, Reggie, let's make it work here in the grass first," she said. "Do you feel your wings? OK, open and close them. Open and close. Open and close.

★ What is the ladybird called?
★ What was the ladybird doing in the air?
★ Why might she be the *best* one to help Reggie?

That's easy, isn't it? Now, up and down. Up and down. Up and down." Stripey was good at giving orders. She was tiny but very strict. And when she looked around, she saw Spikey lifting his paws and Dave performing some great swirling moves with his tail. "You're both gymnasts!" she exclaimed. She was pleased with herself, especially as she had made Reggie smile for the first time. "Do you trust your wings now?" she asked him.

"Yes," Reggie answered proudly.

"Good! Then let's find you a tree so you can jump from a branch."

They all set off together to find the perfect one.

⁓ What questions did the ladybird ask Reggie? What was she
trying to do?

⁓ What do you think of Stripey?

⁓ What do you think Stripey will do now?

Spikey

Soon, they came to a clearing that was surrounded by trees and bushes. In the middle was an old wooden bench with a small tree right behind it.

"Peep, peep, peep, peep, peep," Reggie whistled excitedly as he looked around the little glade. The robin's eyes settled on the tallest tree, which towered above them all, stretching up and up and up towards the sky. He had decided which tree he would be jumping from!

★ What do you think everyone is saying in the picture?
★ Why was Reggie so excited?
★ Do you agree it was right that Reggie should start in a smaller tree?

Spikey

Spikey smiled and thought the little robin was beginning to get more confident now. *That needs building up.* "Why don't you start on this small tree over here?" he suggested. "If you start small and safe, you can go higher as time goes on. I've no doubt that, one day soon, you'll be flying from trees much, much taller than this one. One day, Reggie, but not today."

✒ Why do you think the robin looked at the tallest tree? Was this a good idea?

✒ What are Spikey's hopes for Reggie, both now and in the future?

✒ Spikey said that Reggie should 'start small'. Do you ever start small and build from there? Can you explain your thinking here?

★ Why did Reggie choose to take his friend's and his mum's advice?

★ When was Reggie ready to fly from the tallest tree?

★ What do you think Reggie is thinking in the picture?

Reggie *so* wanted to jump from the tallest tree, but he realised it was much better to follow his friend's advice. Spikey was older and knew much more. *And he's saying what my mum would say if she were here,* Reggie thought, so he decided to play safe.

Dave the worm helped Reggie up onto the bench. Stripey and Spikey said a few words of encouragement as he hopped onto the back of the bench and then up onto a low branch of the small tree behind it. He jumped off, spread his wings and fluttered to the ground. His friends all cheered. So Reggie did it again and again, moving a little higher each time.

After many jumps and flights, he said he was ready for the tallest tree. But when he climbed to the top and looked down, his heart almost stopped. It was a very, very, very long way down!

- What would happen if Reggie had started learning to fly from the tallest tree?
- How did Reggie feel when he reached the top of the tallest tree?
- What advice would you give to young robins who are learning to fly?

Reggie stood tall on a branch, stepping a little to the left and then a little to the right to find the best spot for his jump. Eventually, he launched himself into the air. He found he was falling, despite flapping his wings as hard as he could. He kept flapping so hard: *Flap! Flap! Flap! Flap! Flap! Flap!*

However, nothing was happening. Reggie started to panic. *Why is it all going wrong?* He noticed that his friends on the ground were becoming bigger and he was approaching them very fast. Spikey was moving his paws like they were wings, and Dave was swinging his tail backwards and forwards, both hoping they could somehow help him to fly.

Meanwhile, Stripey was following Reggie on the way down, flapping her own wings in unison with his. "Keep going, Reggie; keep going! Don't give up!" she urged, but still nothing was happening for Reggie.

★ What is happening in the picture?
★ Did Stripey help? How?
★ Is Stripey a good friend? Why?

Spikey

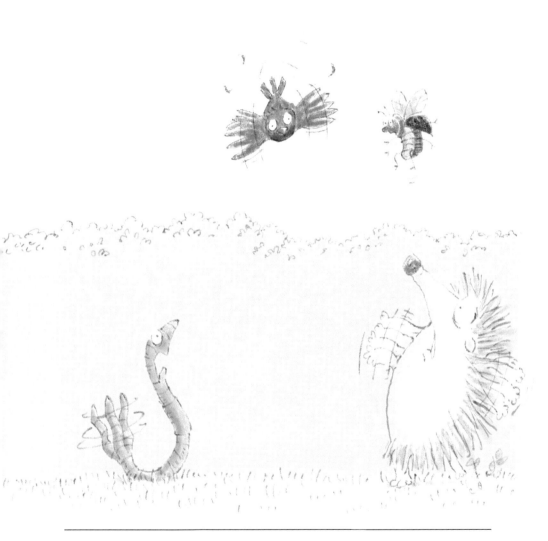

How did Reggie feel when he flapped his wings and nothing happened?

Do you think Reggie should have tried to fly from the top of the tallest tree? Was he ready?

How would you describe a good friend?

★ What does 'hurtling down' mean?

★ Why was Reggie worried about Spikey's spikes?

★ How would you describe what is happening in the picture?

Reggie *did* almost give up – until he realised he was hurtling down towards Spikey's dangerously sharp spikes. *Swish, swish, swish, swish, swish, swish* went his wings. Now the spikes were no longer getting closer. In fact, he started moving gently up and away from them. *Swish! Swish! Swish! Swish! Swish! Swish!*

"*You're flying, Reggie! You're really flying!*" Spikey shouted. He turned to the others. "He's flying, guys. Look, look, look!"

What do the faces of Stripey, Dave, Spikey and Reggie tell you when you look at the picture?

How does Reggie feel when he is flying?

Do you think Reggie was lucky to fly?

They all cheered Reggie until he landed safely back on the branch at the top of the tall tree. He sat next to Stripey, and they high-fived each other.

"Told you!" said Stripey with a big wink.

Reginald was really proud of himself. He lifted off from the branch again and flew above everyone, moving left and right, up and down, back and forth, and round and round and round and round and round and round! He couldn't stop flying. He realised how happy it made him feel.

Everyone could see how easily he was gliding through the air. Spikey was almost jealous. He kept thinking how lovely it must be to be part of the sky. He realised he was still moving his paws as if they were wings: up and down, up and down. This made him smile.

***

If Reggie had paid attention when he was in the air,

★ Why did everyone cheer?

★ Why was Reggie really proud of himself? What do you think he was thinking?

★ How did Tiny show she wanted more food?

he might have seen the park ranger's cottage in the far distance. Tiny, the caterpillar sausage cat, was inside, pestering the park ranger for more food. She had gobbled up her dinner a little while ago and was now pushing her empty bowl around with her nose to show she wanted more.

"Interesting; how interesting! Are you really that hungry, little munchkin?" asked Mr McDougall with a chuckle. He had always been concerned about his beloved animals and whether they ate enough. *No one will ever starve on my watch!* he always thought. He pulled some cat biscuits out of the cupboard in his small, cosy kitchen while Tiny rubbed her head against his legs. He filled up her bowl for a second time and put it down for her to munch. In no time at all, the bowl was empty again. Mr McDougall watched happily as Tiny then walked into the garden with her stomach swinging from side to side.

Why does Reggie keep flying?

What does 'jealous' mean?

What do you think might happen next?

Spikey

Tiny wandered off, looking for a comfy place to lie down. She made her way through the Rose Garden and out towards the big lake in Regent's Park. She crossed a wooden bridge covered by flowering wisteria. It led to a small island in the middle of the lake, which was sometimes used by birdwatchers. On the island was an old tree that she decided to climb. The tree only had a few leaves on it, but she didn't mind. She just wanted a comfortable branch to lie on for a snooze in the early evening sunshine. When she found a branch she liked, it took her a little while to curl up her long, caterpillar-sausage-shaped body. Then she closed her eyes and started purring. All was calm and quiet.

★ How would you describe what is happening in the picture?
★ Where is the tree that Tiny has gone to?
★ Why was Tiny purring?

What do you like about the picture? Why?

Is Tiny being careful? Why do you think that?

What might happen to Tiny now?

★   What is happening in the picture?

★   What was Tiny most scared of?

★   Who can help Tiny? And how?

Spikey

Crack! Craaack! CRAAAAAAAAAAACK!

Tiny opened her eyes in alarm. She hadn't noticed the old tree was dead and its comfortable branches were all rotten – and she had eaten so much that even the biggest branch was going to collapse under her weight! The next moment, she found herself dangling over the lake, clinging on to the broken branch by only her front paws. She could feel the chill of the water below her – and she *hated* water. Most cats don't like to get wet, but this wasn't about getting wet. This was about drowning. She'd never been near deep water before and had no idea how to swim. That meant she was here, all on her own, in danger of falling into the dark lake at any moment. *"Help!"* she screamed. *"Somebody help me. PLEASE!"*

✎ Looking at Tiny's face in the picture, what do you think she is thinking?

✎ Do you feel sorry for Tiny? Why?

✎ Do you think Tiny would help others? Why?

Chapter Five

Reggie was out flying, turning and twisting in the air and enjoying the breath-taking freedom of flight. With his wings, he waved to everyone he could see from high above in the sky. He waved to a squirrel sitting on a pine tree and munching a big nut. He waved to a little mouse that was rustling through some leaves on the ground, and he waved to a big frog sitting on a stone beside the lake. Flying on, he was about to wave to a big animal that appeared to be having fun on the tree that stood on the little island in the middle of the lake when he realised it was Tiny, the caterpillar sausage cat! She was not having fun. He could clearly hear she was crying for help!

He flew over as quickly as he could and sat on the branch that she was clinging to. "Hello, Tiny.

★ Who did Reggie wave to?
★ What is happening in the picture?
★ Would you help Tiny? Why?

What are you doing? What has happened?"

"I was sleeping on this branch, but it broke. I don't know how long I can hang on before I fall into the water. Meeoooow! I *hate* water! Will you please help me, Reggie? *Meeooooow!*"

The robin looked cross. "And why would I do that? The last time we met, you were pinning me down with one of those massive paws you're now using to hang on to that branch. You threatened to eat me. I'm lucky to be alive, to be honest with you."

What are Tiny and Reggie saying to each other in the picture?

Should Reggie help Tiny? Why?

Have you ever helped someone who has been unkind to you? Why?

Tiny looked very ashamed of herself. "Well, yes. I know, I know!" she said. "OK, I wasn't nice to you at all, and I am very, *very* sorry! Will you please help me now, though? I don't know how much time I have left."

"Hmm...well...maybe! But I need you to promise that you won't catch me or *any other bird* from now on. There you have it! You need to give me this promise. You have plenty of food at home, and you're well looked after, so you don't need to eat birds as well, *do you?*" Reggie waved his wings urgently and hopped along his branch to stand right beside the cat. She looked enormous!

"OK, OK! You have my promise. Just help me now, please; *please!* Meeooow!" Tiny felt she was losing her grip on the branch. She started whimpering in fear.

"All right, all right!" *How can I save this*

★   Why was Tiny ashamed?
★   What did Reggie ask Tiny to promise?
★   Do you think Tiny will keep her promise?

cat? Reggie looked at her and saw the fear in her wide eyes. "Tiny, please hang on just a little longer. I'll fetch my friends."

Reggie flew off as quickly as he could, looking for Spikey and his friends, but he was starting to get really, really tired. He had been flying non-stop since he had begun to learn, and he was now desperate for a break. Using almost the last of his failing strength, he flew back to where he'd left his friends, shouting Spikey's name.

"I'm here; right here," Spikey called back, waving at the little robin. Then he watched in dismay as Reggie dropped like a stone, hit the ground and sat without moving, gasping for breath. Spikey rushed over. "What's wrong? Are you OK?"

"Yes…er…no!" Reggie wheezed. "I need your help! All of you; I need *all* of you! Branch…cat…water…*now!*"

- Should Tiny be ashamed of hunting a bird? Why?
- Why is Reggie so tired?
- What do you think will happen next?

Spikey looked at the others with a puzzled frown. Reggie had been away for just a little while, and it looked like something bad had happened. "Reggie, slow down! Tell us exactly what's going on."

The robin took a very deep breath. "You know Tiny...Tiny, the caterpillar sausage cat? She's got herself into a terrible pickle and needs our help. Hurry up! She really, *really* needs us!"

"Why should we 'elp 'er, Reggie? The last time we saw 'er, she was goin' to eat ya! 'Ave ya forgotten that, mate?" said Dave, looking very confused.

"But, but, but...she's about to fall into the water, and she gave me her promise not to catch any more birds – *ever!* So can you please come with me now and help her?" Reggie begged, waving his wings.

The friends looked at each other and nodded in agreement. Then they rushed off through the park.

★ What is happening in the picture? Why?
★ What does 'got herself into a terrible pickle' mean?
★ Why is Dave unsure about helping Tiny?

Spikey

Stripey flew with Reggie and guided Spikey from the air by telling the little hedgehog which way to go. Dave took a shortcut underground as he had been to the lake many times before. He and Spikey bumped into each other as they arrived at the bridge together.

"Sorry, guv," said Dave. "Do you fink we're doin' the right fing 'ere?"

"Of course we are. We should always help anyone who's in trouble." Spikey was surprised the worm was asking him such a question.

Is it a good idea for Reggie to trust Tiny and her promise?

Did Reggie and his friends find it easy to get back to Tiny? Why?

Does Dave want to help Tiny? What is he thinking? And what do you think of Dave?

Soon, they were all standing next to the rotten, old tree on the island, looking up at Tiny dangling in the air.

"What do we do now?" asked Reggie, speaking everyone's thoughts.

Spikey looked around and spotted a small boat nearby on the opposite shoreline. "Reggie, do you see that boat? Have you got the strength to fly over there and check if it's moored?"

Reggie didn't waste a single second. He flew the few metres over the water and shouted back, *"Yes, it's tied up, but I think I can undo it with my beak."* He pecked and pecked at the rope as hard as he could, but it remained tied. His beak hadn't grown strong enough just yet. He looked in despair at his friends across the water.

But just when they all thought everything was lost, Spikey suddenly caught a glimpse of Mr Fox's tail in the distance and realised help was at hand.

★ What did Spikey ask Reggie to do?
★ What are White Tip and Reggie doing in the picture?
★ Why does Reggie fluff up?

"White Tip!" he called. "It is so good to see you! Will you please help Reggie to undo this rope? We're in the middle of a rescue mission, you see, and we desperately need this boat here."

White Tip smiled at Spikey and nodded. He then carefully approached Reggie who looked really small, even though he'd managed to fluff himself up. The fox didn't want to scare Reggie off, so he turned aside and tucked his sharp teeth into the rope to start chewing. Within a few moments, it became loose, and he was able to pull the knot undone. He looked at Reggie. "Coming with me?" he asked.

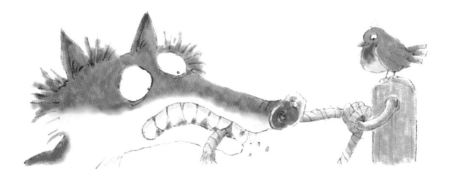

Why did Reggie look in despair across the water?

Why did White Tip behave carefully when he was near Reggie?

What do you think Reggie was thinking as White Tip chewed on the rope?

Reggie was still fluffed up, but he jumped quickly into the boat, making sure he was far away from White Tip. He had never seen a fox before, and he wanted to be on the safe side. The current in the lake did the rest. The boat floated slowly towards Tiny, who was still swinging in the air, her claws and paws throbbing with pain.

"Guys, you're the best!" Spikey shouted proudly. "Over to you now, Tiny. You just need to wait another few moments and then drop right into the boat."

★ What is happening in the picture?
★ How did Tiny feel? Why?
★ What do you think will happen next?

Tiny was tired, frightened and really didn't want to take any chances with getting wet, but she still felt uneasy. "How do I know I can trust you?" she asked.

Dave the worm slithered along the branch from which Tiny was dangling, gripped it with his strong tail and leaned down so his face was right opposite hers. "Look, ya can either trust us an' do exactly what we tell ya, or ya can just fall into the water. It's yer choice! I'm a great measurer, as ya all know, an' Spikey is quite right. We just need to let the current straighten the boat a little bit more...Yes! 'Ere we go! When I say 'free', ya just let go. One...two...*free!*"

- How do you think Reggie felt as he was sitting in a boat with a fox, going to save Tiny the cat?
- What did Tiny think of the plan to drop into the boat?
- What do you think of the choices Dave gave to Tiny? Do you think she'll trust him?

Spikey

As Dave said it, Tiny did it! She fell right into the middle of the boat, landing on all four of her paws. Tiny couldn't believe that she was safe and sound and dry. As the boat drifted close to the shore, the exhausted cat tried to jump out. She got her front paws onto the grass, but her limp body and back legs were still in the boat, which made it drift backwards again. Tiny had to stretch until she was way too long – definitely a caterpillar sausage cat!

Reggie was watching everything from the air. "Spikey, Spikey! We need more help!"

They all rushed over to grab Tiny's front paws. She was now fully stretched between the bank and the boat, her tabby body looking like a little bridge.

They managed to pull her and the boat back towards the shore, and White Tip rushed from the back of the boat to help push the tired cat to safety.

★ How did Tiny feel when she was in the boat?
★ Why was Tiny so tired and exhausted?
★ What is happening in the picture?

✧ Why was Tiny struggling to get out of the boat?

✧ Can you see any friendship and trust in the picture?

✧ What do you think will happen next?

Chapter Six

Along the shoreline, Tiny was checking and cleaning herself, not quite believing she had really made it to safety without getting wet. She looked around and discovered she was surrounded by Spikey and his friends. "Thank you, Spikey, and thank you, Reggie. I wouldn't have made it without you all!"

There was a short silence, which was broken by Reggie: "Oh, I am *sooo* tired!" He yawned.

Stripey, who was sitting on Spikey's head, laughed out loud. "Flying takes time and energy, little robin, but you'll sleep the tiredness off and will be fine tomorrow for a new adventure with us!"

"Thank you, Stripey, that's good to know." Reggie turned to Spikey. "Thank you too. You're such a great friend! You have taught me how to fly, and without

---

★   Was Tiny happy? Why?

★   Was it Reggie who saved Tiny?

★   Why did Reggie suddenly decide to go home? Do you agree with his reasons?

you doing that, I wouldn't have saved this cat here!" Clearly, the little robin still believed he was in charge of the world and had forgotten all about teamwork. "I'll now go home because I need to tell my brothers and sisters what has happened – and how brave I was!"

Spikey smiled, feeling very happy. "Stripey, here, will fly with you and make sure you get home safe and sound. I believe your nest is on Stripey's way home anyway."

The little ladybird nodded in agreement and flew off with Reggie, waving everyone goodbye.

***

Do you think Tiny has made new friends?

Why did Spikey and his friends stay with Tiny and not leave her?

Why do you think Stripey flew home with Reggie?

As the two small figures disappeared into the distance, Tiny turned to the others with a shy and gentle smile. "Thank you, everyone. You didn't have to help me, but you did. Even though I really wanted to hurt little Reggie, you all still came to save me. How can I ever repay you?"

★　What is happening in the picture?

★　Does Tiny feel sorry for what she did?

★　Why was White Tip so firm with Tiny?

White Tip looked at Spikey and Dave, and then took charge. "I'm sure it isn't just me who is hungry now, Tiny. You live with the park ranger, don't you? That means you'll be given your bedtime snack soon by Mr McDougall, and knowing you, there will be more than just one dish. So…I think we all deserve to join the party!"

What different feelings can you see in the picture?

Why does White Tip look so angry in the picture?

What is 'the party' that White Tip talks about?

Spikey

Tiny nodded slowly and sighed sadly. She really was too greedy to share her lovely, plentiful food, but she also felt like she had no choice. She owed her friends everything, especially White Tip.

They all headed to Mr McDougall's cottage, and when they arrived, there were already some dishes full of tasty cat food waiting. Tiny looked around and waved at them to come from around the corner where they were hiding. The coast was clear, so they all nipped in and started eating.

"Shh, Spikey, shhhh!" exclaimed Tiny. "Learn some manners. You can't eat this noisily. Everyone will hear us!" The cat was astonished as she had never shared a meal with a hedgehog before.

"Sorry! I-I-I will try my best, but hedgehogs aren't polite eaters. We're famous for making a noise while dining out." Spikey was a little embarrassed.

★ What is happening in the picture?
★ How is Spikey behaving?
★ What does 'learn some manners' mean?

What is Tiny thinking and feeling in the picture?

What does 'the coast was clear' mean?

What question would you ask other readers about this page?

"And where's Dave? I can't deal with any more trouble," snapped Tiny. She was getting a little bit cross with her new companions.

"I'm 'ere! This is wonderful, absolutely wonderful!" called Dave, sticking his head out of a massive pile of compost. The next moment, he was gone again to enjoy another swim between the rotting greenery and the soil.

Spikey, White Tip and Tiny finished every scrap of food in the bowls.

Spikey sat down afterwards and rubbed his little tummy. "That was amazing, Tiny! Thank you so much for letting us eat with you."

"Well, I guess it's time to say goodbye now the day is done," said White Tip; he looked ready to set off to roam the night like he always did.

"Oh, yes. I always forget you have to leave in

★ What is Dave doing in the picture?
★ How do you think Dave feels in the picture? Why?
★ Why does White Tip say goodbye?

the evening," Spikey replied a little sadly. Dusk was his least favourite part of the day. It was the time when he had to say goodbye to everyone and stay on his own again. Then he saw Tiny wandering off alone too. "Hey! Where are you going?" he called to the cat.

✲ Why is Tiny a little bit cross? Is she right?

✲ What is 'dusk'? Why does Spikey not like it?

✲ Where does White Tip go at night?

"I'm going indoors to lie on my soft cushion right next to the fireplace. It was hard work demolishing my dish of food, so I need to have a good rest and catch up on some beauty sleep," Tiny answered importantly.

"Oh, I see…" Spikey looked at White Tip. They were both a bit jealous Tiny had the luxury of a soft cushion in a warm part of the house.

She walked away, and they watched her reach the door and turn to look back at them to say goodbye. But Tiny caught sight of Spikey's sad little eyes. "Where are *you* going, Spikey?"

"Oh…er…I'll find something nearby. I just need a small, warm hole with soft leaves to be cosy." He was also very tired; in fact, the idea of having to go to look for a safe place to sleep was very worrying.

★   Where is Tiny going? Why?
★   Why did Spikey have 'sad little eyes'?
★   What is Tiny doing in the picture? Why?

Spikey

"Do you mean something like this?" Tiny asked, pointing towards a big pile of logs and branches in the corner of Mr McDougall's garden.

"Oh wow! That looks really comfy and nice!" cried Spikey, and he scampered towards the log pile.

Tiny followed him and pointed to a hole at the bottom. "This is where you get in, and ta-dah! There's a little cave inside."

*★ What is a 'beauty sleep'?

*★ On page 90, do you think Spikey knows where he will sleep tonight? How must he feel?

*★ How does Tiny help Spikey? What do you think Tiny is thinking and feeling?

"Wow!" gasped Spikey. The cave looked a bit like a cosy hedgehog nest. "Do you think I may stay in it?"

"Well, you know, it's my little hideout, but I guess I can lend it to you for...for...just tonight!" As a cat, Tiny was battling against her selfish nature and didn't want to let go of anything easily. "I can always pop in later to see how you are, maybe?"

"Oh yes! That would be just wonderful, if you could," said Spikey with a huge smile. "Then I won't be all alone for the whole night."

"I wondered...er...if I could fit in too?" White Tip wanted to know. "Just in case I get my nightly business done early, you see."

"*Sure thing!*" shouted Spikey; he was already inside and turning round and round to make himself comfortable. The moment his head hit the leaves, he was asleep and making cute little hedgehog snoring noises.

★ Why did Spikey like the cave?
★ Why did Tiny join Spikey and White Tip in the cave?
★ Why couldn't Tiny settle down to sleep?

Spikey

Tiny stood together with White Tip outside the cave as she waited for him to leave on his nightly forage around the park. But now the moment had come, the fox didn't want to go. He was also incredibly tired after everything that had happened earlier, and with his tummy full of cat food, he didn't need to find anything else to eat either. "Please may I go in now?" he asked politely. "It looks so cosy and safe…"

"Of course," Tiny replied, "and I'll join you as well. I can't leave you two in there on your own."

It was a bit of a squeeze, but the cat and the fox – once unsure about each other if ever they met, but now good friends – managed to snuggle in either side of Spikey without waking him or scratching themselves on his sharp spines. They closed their eyes, but Tiny couldn't settle straight away because Spikey was now snoring at full volume.

Hedgehogs! she thought.

- Who and what do you imagine Spikey was thinking about when he saw the cosy cave?
- Why did White Tip want to sleep in the cave too?
- Are cats and foxes usually friends?

★ What is happening in the picture?
★ What is a 'racket'? Why is Tiny complaining?
★ What is it like in that cave just now?

Later in the night, Tiny woke up. "How can you sleep in this racket?" she grumbled.

White Tip, who had been woken up by the noise too, showed her what to do: "You can use your paws to cover your ears."

Tiny had never done this before, but when she tried, she found it worked! She didn't hear a thing. Tiny curled her long caterpillar-sausage-cat body into a ball, closed her bright-green eyes and was soon fast asleep again.

✸ What is Tiny thinking in the picture? Does she look like a happy cat?

✸ Why has Tiny never used her paws to cover her ears before?

✸ If you heard Spikey honking away in his sleep, what would you do?

White Tip opened one eye again and saw Spikey had now started twitching, clearly having a dream. The fox smiled. *I've been watching him all the time, and what a day he's had! He found a new friend in the little robin and helped to teach him to fly. While doing that, he also managed to find two other animals that seem to be friendly enough to join our gang. Tiny even shared her meal with us...* White Tip yawned in the middle of his thinking. Spikey was now making noises as well

---

★ Was White Tip with Spikey the whole day?

★ What was Spikey dreaming about?

★ Who was having the same dream as Spikey?

as twitching his paws, and White Tip realised that, in his dreams, his little friend was flying! Spikey was moving his front paws as if they were wings. Hedgehog wings. And then he looked at Tiny, who wasn't curled up in a big ball any more. *Ha ha ha. Tiny is twitching too – she's flying as well! They are both dreaming about flying with Reggie!* And with that, he fell asleep.

Do you dream when you are asleep? Do you remember your dreams? And what is the most amazing dream you have ever had?

Why was White Tip watching Spikey the whole day?

What do you think of White Tip now?

When Dave popped up through a hole in the floor, everyone was twitching and smiling with happiness in their sleep. *Unbelievable! I'm so glad I ain't got paws or wings meself. At least I can sleep peaceful-like!* he thought. Then he snuggled down between Spikey and Tiny and fell asleep himself. He snored and twitched a little, then started making swirling movements.

Later that night, by the light of a full moon, two small creatures flew over the roof of Mr McDougall's cottage and landed on top of the log pile.

"They're not here, Reggie," said Stripey, looking round at the empty garden. "May we go back now?" She was cross about being woken up and asked to escort the robin back to the place they had left not so long ago. After a short sleep, the little robin had missed his new friends so much that he couldn't wait for morning to be with them again.

★ What is happening in the picture?
★ What is a full moon?
★ What have you learned from this book?

✷ Why did Dave, Stripey and Reggie look for their friends?

✷ What do you think Reggie and Stripey are saying in the picture?

✷ Were you inspired by this book? If so, how?

★ What is happening in the picture?
★ Why is Reggie proud?
★ Before you turn the page, what do you think you will see in the next picture?

"Listen!" said Reggie excitedly. "I can hear snoring. It's coming from underneath us."

Fluttering down, Reggie and Stripey found the entrance to the cave and peeped inside. They saw their friends all fast asleep and twitching about. Spikey, White Tip and Tiny were all moving their paws like wings, and Dave was making swirling moves with his tail as they slept soundly, tucked up together.

Reggie stuck out his fluffy, red breast with pride. "They're all dreaming about flying." he said. "They all want to be like *me!* Some robins *do* rule the world. This is a flying hedgehog gang indeed!"

But Stripey wasn't listening. She had already flown inside and was settling down for the night with the others.

"Hey! Wait for me!" called Reggie.

Why does Reggie think that some robins rule the world?

Has Spikey's shorter back leg ever made a difference?

What do you think will happen to Spikey and his friends in their next adventure?

The questions in this book have been further informed by conversations with Emeritus Professor Irvine Gersch, who is an expert on spiritual listening, listening to the voice of the child, and asking meaningful and insightful questions to further promote children's thinking and learning.

If you have enjoyed answering the questions at the bottom of the pages, you can find more on Spikey's own website. It also has lots of facts about hedgehogs, which are truly amazing.
Visit www.thelittlehedgehog.com.

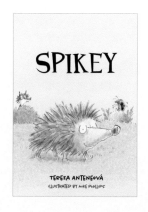

Further information about hedgehogs and how to support them

In response to the worrying decline of hedgehogs across the UK, People's Trust for Endangered Species (PTES) and The British Hedgehog Preservation Society (BHPS) launched the Hedgehog Street campaign, which seeks to conserve this iconic species and empower the British public to help hedgehogs in their own gardens. By encouraging natural insect food or linking up your gardens with 'hedgehog highways', you can help hedgehogs. PTES and BHPS are also currently commissioning various research projects into the reasons for the decline of hedgehogs and measures that could be taken to reverse the effects.

It's all about giving people an understanding of hedgehogs, why they are declining and how easy it is to help them. With their unique, charismatic and curious appearance, hedgehogs regularly feature as 'Britain's favourite wild mammal' in polls and evoke such an affectionate response from the public that there's every reason to be genuinely hopeful that we can reverse this decline.

Hedgehogs love gardens, and we know what features they need to survive and thrive in suburbia. Hedgehog Street is all about simple things everyone can do to help save our favourite wild animal. If you want to join us in the fight to save this national treasure, sign up to Hedgehog Street today at www.hedgehogstreet.org.

About the Author

Tereza Hepburn

As a girl, Tereza lived in a small village just outside one of the castles of Prague, Czechoslovakia (now in the Czech Republic), next to an old wood and a gentle, flowing stream. She and her father spent long summer days lying in the grass, watching the wildlife, and telling each other stories about the lives, hopes and dreams of all the animals they saw. Soon, the world of Spikey and all his friends was born.

Later, Tereza and her family moved to England, and after a few years, she missed Spikey and his friends, so they all moved back to the Czech Republic again.

Tereza grew up. She worked hard and became a journalist, a newsreader and a political reporter, allowing her to tell different stories to the whole wide world.

However, London kept calling to Tereza. Soon, she moved back to this beautiful, ancient and vibrant city that's so full of stories, and she now lives in Islington with her husband John and their two cats: Meowglish and Johnson. Everyone is now a Hepburn, and as you might know, Hepburns always have many more stories to tell.